The Giant and the Frippit

Linda Strachan

Illustrated by James Cotton

Rigby

At the top of a tree
lived a small, brown frippit.
At the bottom of the tree
lived a giant.

The giant was a good giant.

He liked all the animals in the woods.

All the animals liked him.

But the frippit didn't like the animals.

The frippit didn't like the good giant.

Oh, no!

One day he ran down the tree, and took the giant's picnic.

The giant looked for his picnic,
but he couldn't find it.

The giant looked in the frippit's house.

"Did you take my picnic?" asked the giant.

"No," said the frippit. "I didn't."

BUT HE DID!

The next day, the frippit
ran down the tree
and took the giant's book.

The giant looked for his book,
but he couldn't find it.

The giant looked in the frippit's house.
"Did you take my book?"
asked the giant.
"No," said the frippit. "I didn't."

BUT HE DID!

That night the wind blew and blew.
The wind shook the tree,
and the frippit fell out of his house.

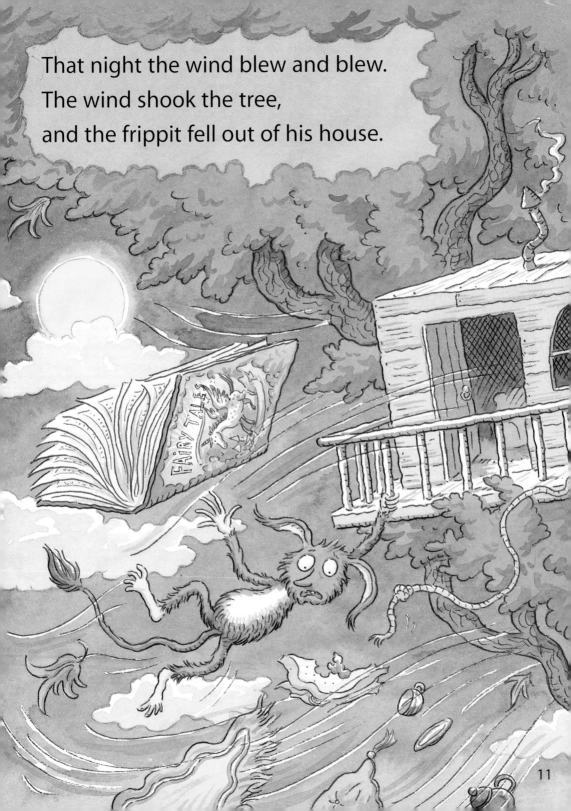

He fell
all the way
down
to the foot
of
the
tree.

FAIRY TALES

"Help!" he said.

The giant saw the frippit falling.

He put out his hand,

and the frippit fell into it.

The giant took the frippit into his house.

The giant gave the frippit some food.
Then he put the frippit to bed
and read him a story.
"I'm sorry I took your book,"
said the frippit.
"And I'm sorry I took your picnic."

From that day on,
the giant and the frippit
were good friends.